POWER OF THE HOLY SPIRIT.

TO MY LOVELY MOTHER, MISS NAKAMYA JOSEPHINE AND MISS NANDAWULA MARGRET I PRAY FOR GOD'S BLESSINGS UPON THEM.

CONTENTS

CHAPTER 1

HOLY SPIRIT

He is called holy because his job is primarily internal. When we receive the holy Spirit, he comes and gives us new hearts then we become holy. To receive the spirit is to receive a helper and advocate for the soul.

32 NAMES OF THE SPIRIT.

- **HOLY SPIRIT**

Do not cast me away from your presence, and do not take your Holy Spirit from me. **Psalm 51:11 Luke 11:13**. If you then being evil, know how to give good gifts to your children, how much more will your heavenly father give the Holy Spirit those who ask him!''

- **ETERNAL SPIRIT**

How much more shall the blood of Christ, who through the eternal Spirit offered himself without spot to God, cleanse your conscience from dead works to serve the living God? **Hebrews 9:14.**

- **THE COMFORTER AND HELPER.**

He is also called our comforter. **John 14:16**. And I will pray the father, and he will give you another helper, that he may abide with you forever.

- **SPIRIT OF TRUTH.**

The spirit of truth, whom the world cannot receive, because it neither sees him nor knows him; but you know him, for he dwells with you and will be in you. **John 14:17**

- **GENEROUS /GOOD SPIRIT**

Restore to me the Joy of your salvation, and uphold me by your generous spirit. **Psalm 51:12.**

- **GOOD SPIRIT**

Nehemiah 9:20. You also gave your good Spirit to instruct them, and did not withhold your manna from their mouth, and gave them water for their thirst.

- **SPIRIT OF COUNSEL**

Isaiah 11:2. The Spirit of the LORD shall rest upon him, the spirit of wisdom and understanding, the spirit of counsel and might, the spirit of knowledge and of the fear of the LORD.

- **SPIRIT OF GOD**

For what man knows the things of a man except the spirit of the man which is in him? Even so no one knows the things of God except the spirit of God. **1 Corinthians 2:11.**

- **SPIRIT OF BURNING**

When the Lord has washed away the filth of the daughters of Zion, and purged the blood of Jerusalem from her midst, by the spirit of judgment and by the spirit of burning.

- **SPIRIT OF THE SON.**

Galatians 4:6. And because you are sons, God has sent forth the spirit of his son into your hearts, crying out, Abba, Father!"

- **SPIRIT OF WISDOM AND REVELATION.**

Ephesians 1:17. That the God of our Lord ,Jesus Christ, the father of glory, may give to you the spirit of wisdom and revelation in the knowledge of him.

- **SPIRIT OF GRACE**

Also the Holy Spirit can be called the spirit of grace. **Zechariah 12:10**. And I will pour on the house of David and on the house of the inhabitants of Jerusalem the spirit of grace and supplication; then they will look on me whom they pierced. Yes, they will mourn for him as one mourns for his only son, and grieve for him as one grieves for a first born.

- **SPIRIT OF PROPHECY.**

The Holy Spirit is also called the spirit of prophecy. Revelation 19:10. And I fell at his feet to worship him. But he said to me; see that you do not do that! I am your fellow servant, and of your brethren who have the testimony of Jesus. Worship God! For the testimony of Jesus, is the spirit of prophecy."

7 SYMBOLS OF THE HOLY SPIRIT.

The Holy Spirit is presented with some symbols in the Bible, which depict reality of truth about the Holy Spirit.

- **THE HOLY SPIRIT COMES AS RAIN.**

JOEL 2:23-29. Be glad then, you children of Zion, and rejoice in the LORD your God; for he has given you the former rain faithfully, and he will cause the rain to come down for you the former rain and the latter rain in the first month. The threshing floors shall be full of wheat, and the vats shall overflow with new wine and oil. "So I will restore to you the years that the swarming locust has eaten, the crawling locust, the consuming locust' and the chewing locust, my great army which I sent among you. You shall eat in plenty and be satisfied, and praise the name of the LORD your God, who has dealt wondrously with you; and my people, shall never be put to shame. Then you shall know that I am in the midst of Israel: I am the LORD your God and there is no other. My people shall never be put to shame. And it shall come to pass afterward that I will pour out my Spirit on all flesh; your sons and your daughters shall prophesy, your old men shall dream dreams, your young men shall see visions. And also on my menservants I will pour out my Spirit in those days.

- **THE HOLY SPIRIT COMES AS RIVERS.**

JOHN 7:37-39. On the last day, that great day of the feast, Jesus stood and cried out, saying, "if anyone thirsts, let him come to me and drink. He who believes in me, as the scripture has said, out of his heart will flow rivers of living water." But this he spoke concerning the spirit, whom those believing in him would receive; for the Holy Spirit was not yet given, because Jesus was not yet glorified. Who is he?

- **THE HOLY SPIRIT COMES AS WIND**

The wind blows where it wishes, and you hear the sound of it, but cannot tell where it comes from and where it goes. So is everyone who is born of the spirit." **John 3:8**

- **THE HOLY SPIRIT COMES AS OIL**

Acts 10:38 . How God anointed Jesus of Nazareth with the Holy Spirit and with power, who went about doing good and healing all who were oppressed by the devil, for God was with him.1 John 2:20.But you are an anointing from the Holy one, and you know all things.

- **THE HOLY SPIRIT COMES AS WINE.**

Ephesians 5:18. And do not be drunk with wine, in which is dissipation; but be filled with the Spirit.

- **THE HOLY SPIRIT COMES AS FIRE**

ACTS 2:3-4 . Then there appeared to them divided tongues, as of fire, and one sat upon each of them. And they were all filled with the Holy Spirit and began to speak with other tongues, as the spirit gave them utterance.

- **THE HOLY SPIRIT COMES AS A DOVE**

Matthew 3:16. When he had been baptized, Jesus came up immediately from the water; and behold, the heavens were opened to him, and he saw the spirit of God descending like a dove and lighting upon him. A Dove symbolizes peace. Psalms 55:6; purity [song of songs 5:2;6:9]; innocence[Matt. 10:16]; and beauty[song of Solomon 1:15; 2:14].

- **A SEAL**

The Holy Spirit can be seen as a seal. **Ephesians 1:13-14** says, In him you trusted, after you heard the word of truth, the gospel of salvation; in whom also, having believed, you were sealed with the Holy Spirit of promise, who is the guarantee of our inheritance until the redemption of the purchased possession, to the praise of his glory.

- **AS A GUARANTEE**

2 Corinthians 1:20-22. For all the promises of God in him is yes, and in him Amen, to the glory of God through us. Now he who establishes us with you in Christ and has anointed us is God, who also has sealed us and given us the spirit in our hearts as a guarantee.

7 MARKS OF THE HOLY SPIRIT IN A PERSON.

According to **1 Samuel 10:6**, it is clear that when man receives the Holy Spirit, he changes. It says, and then the spirit of the LORD will come upon you, and be turned into another man. **Ephesians 5:18.** And do not be drunk with wine, in which is dissipation; but be filled with the spirit, speaking to one another in Psalms and hymns and spiritual songs, singing and making melody in your heart to the Lord, giving thanks always for all things to God the father in the name of our Lord Jesus Christ, submitting to one another in the fear of God.

- **CONFIDENCE**

Romans 15:13. Now may the God of hope fill you with all joy and peace in believing, that you may abound in hope by the power of the Holy Spirit.

- **BOLDNESS**

One of the things that show that a person has the gift of the Holy Spirit is boldness. **Acts 4:29-31.** Now Lord, look on their threats, and grant to your servants that with all boldness they may speak your word, by stretching out your hand to heal, and that signs and wonders may be done through the name of your holy servant Jesus." And when they had prayed, the place where they were assembled together was shaken; and they were all filled with the Holy Spirit, and they spoke the word of God with boldness.

- **AUTHORITY**

God gives us the authority when we get the Holy Spirit. Acts 10:38.How God anointed Jesus of Nazareth with the Holy Spirit and with power, who were oppressed by the devil, for God was with him.

- **BURDEN FOR THE LOST**

You can have the burden for the lost**. Acts 1:8.** But you shall receive power when the Holy Spirit has come upon you; and you shall be witnesses to me in Jerusalem, and in all Judea and Samaria, and to the end of the earth.''

- **GENEROSITY**

Romans 12:6-8. Having then gifts differing according to the grace that is given to us then let us use them: if prophecy, let us prophesy in proportion to our faith; or ministry, let us use it in our ministering; he who teaches, in exhortation; he who gives, with liberality; he who leads, with diligence; he who shows mercy, with cheerfulness.

- **REVELATION.**

Most people receive revelations and this is a sign of having the gift of the Holy Spirit**. John 14:26.** But the helper, the Holy Spirit, whom the father will send in my name, he will teach you all things, and bring to your remembrance all things that I said to you.

FRUITS OF THE SPIRIT

- **LOVE**

Love is one of the fruits of the spirit. If a person is guided by the Holy Spirit, that person will spread love to everyone even to his/her enemies. You get that unconditional love. **Galatians 5:22.**

- **WORD OF WISDOM.**

When you get wisdom, you get solutions. **1 Corinthians 12:7-8**. But the manifestation of the spirit is given to each one for the profit of all: for to one is given the word of wisdom through the spirit, to another the word of knowledge through the same spirit.

- **WORD OF KNOWLEDGE.**

Knowledge is one of the prophetic gifts**. 1 Corinthians 12:7-8**. But the manifestation of the spirit is given to each one for the profit of all: for to one is given the word of wisdom through the spirit, to another the word of knowledge through the same spirit.

- **PEACE**

The Holy Spirit also gives peace to those who follow God's commandments. Peace is one of the fruits of the spirit according to **Galatians 5:22.**

- **PROPHECY.**

The Holy Spirit gives the people the spirit of Prophecy. 1 Corinthians 12:10. Mark 8:31.

- **LONG SUFFERING.**

It's hard to bear with the longsuffering. The Holy Spirit guides you on how to endure the pain and how to leave with the longsuffering in life without hating your life. **Galatians 5:22.**

- **FAITHFULNESS.**

When you are guided with the Holy Spirit, you get the fruit of faith. **Galatians 5:22.**

- **KINDNESS**

Not all people are kind. People who get the fruits of the Holy Spirit, also get the fruit of kindness. Galatians 5:22.

- **SELF-CONTROL.**

Self-control is also a fruit of the Holy Spirit. **Galatians 5:23**

- **GENTLENESS**

The Spirit helps us to get the fruit of gentleness**. Galatians 5:23.**

- **DISCERNMENT**

For this case, you have a gift to see the spirit.**1 Corinthians 12:10.** To another the working of miracles, to another prophecy, to another discerning of spirits, to another different kinds of tongues, to another the interpretation of tongues.

- **INSIGHT**

For this, you see the souls and thoughts**.1 Corinthians 14:24-25.** Jesus had the fruit of insight. Matthew 12:25 says, But Jesus knew their thoughts, and said to them:'' Every kingdom divided against itself is brought to desolation, and every city or house divided against itself will not stand.

HOW TO RECEIVE THE HOLY SPIRIT.

- **READ THE BIBLE**

Get a bible and begin to read. Check into the bible on what you can do to receive the Holy Spirit. **Acts 2:38**. Then Peter said to them, " Rent, and let every one of you be baptized in the name of Jesus Christ for the remission of sins; and you shall receive the gift of the Holy Spirit.

- **REPENT.**

You have to repent of your sins. Every sin inside of you is preventing you from experiencing the fullness of God and if you will repent of your sins believe the blood of Jesus washed them away and ask Jesus to become part and live inside of you. When you repent of your sins, God can give you the gift of Holy Spirit.

- **BAPTISM**

When you get baptized, you can receive the gift of the Holy Spirit. **John 1:32-34**. And John bore witness, saying, "I saw the spirit descending from heaven like a dove, and he remained upon him. I did not know him, but he who sent me to baptize with water said to me, 'Upon whom you see the spirit descending, and remaining on him, this is he who baptizes with the Holy Spirit.' And I have seen and testified that this is the son of God." **John 3:5-8**. Jesus answered, "Most assuredly, I say to you, unless one is born of water and the Spirit, he cannot enter the kingdom of God. That which is born of the flesh is flesh, and that which is born again.' The wind blows where it wishes, and you hear the sound of it, but cannot tell where it comes from and where it goes. So is everyone who is born of the spirit."

- **ASK GODTO GIVE YOU THE HOLY SPIRIT.**

When you ask God for something, he will give it to you**. Luke 11:9-10**. "So I say to you, ask, and it will be given to you; seek, and you will find; knock, and it will be opened to you. For everyone who asks receives, and he who seeks finds, and to him who knocks it will be opened. **LUKE 11:13**.If you then, being evil, know how to give good gifts to your children, how much more will your heavenly father give the Holy Spirit to those who ask him!"

- **LIVE A GOOD CHRISTIAN LIFE.**

We have to live a good Christian life. Repay no one evil for evil. Have regard for good things in the sight of all men. If it is possible, as much as depends on you, live peaceably with all men. Beloved, do not avenge yourselves, but rather give place to wrath; for it is written, vengeance is mine, I will repay," says the Lord. Therefore "if your enemy is hungry, feed him; If he is thirsty, give him a drink; for in so doing you will heap coals of fire on his head." Do not be overcome by evil, but overcome evil with good. **Roman 12:17-21**. **Galatians 5:24-26.** And those who are

Christ's have crucified the fresh with its passions and desires. If we live in the spirit, let us also walk in the Spirit. Let us not become conceited, provoking one another, envying one another. **Roman 12:14-16**. Bless those who persecute you; bless and do not curse. Rejoice with those who rejoice, and weep with those who weep. Be of the same mind toward one another. Do not set your mind on high things, but associate with the humble. Do not be wise in your own opinion.

- **PRAY TO GOD.**

Pray to God and he will give you the gift of the Holy Spirit. Romans 12:12-13. Rejoicing in hope, patient in tribulation, continuing steadfastly in prayer, distributing to the needs of the saints, given to hospitality.

HOW TO SURRENDER TO THE HOLY SPIRIT

- **ACT IN FAITH.**

God wants us to have faith in him. Therefore we can surrender to the Holy Spirit by acting in faith. According to **Hebrews 11:1-3**, Faith is the substance of things hoped for, the evidence of things hoped for, the evidence of things not seen. For by it the elders obtained a good testimony. By faith we understand that the worlds were framed by the word of things which are seen were not made of things which are visible. So it's important for us to act in faith.

- **LIVE IN REPENTENCE.**

The Holy Spirit is holy, so we are also supposed to be holy. Therefore it's important for us to live a repentance life. According to **1 John 1:9-10,** it says, If we confess our sins, he is faithful and just to forgive us our sins and to cleanse us from all unrighteous. If we say that we have not sinned, we make him a liar, and his word is not in us.

- **REVERENCE/OBEY HIS WORD**

Reverencing the Holy Spirit is like obeying to the Holy Spirit. Therefore listen to his voice and don't grieve him. How quickly do you respond when he speaks? Answering on time is obedience but delay is disobedient. Respect his words, therefore honor him and obey him. Love him, obey him and trust him.

If you reverence the words of the Holy Spirit, then you are surrendering to the Holy Spirit. **ISAIAH 66:2,** says, for all those things my hand has made, and all those things exist," says the LORD. " But on this one will I look: on him whom is poor and of contrite Spirit, and who trembles at my word.

- **BE MINDFUL OF HIS PRESENCE.**

Our bodies are the temple of the Holy Spirit so we have to be mindful if we want to surrender to the Holy Spirit. **1 Corinthians 6:15-19**. Do you not know that your bodies are members of Christ? Shall I then take the members of Christ and make the members of a harlot? Certainly not! Or do you not know that he who is joined to a harlot is one body with her? For the two," He says, "shall become one flesh." But he who is joined to the Lord is one spirit with him. Flee sexual immorality. Every sin that a man does is outside the body, but he who commits sexual immorality sins against his own body. Or do you not know that your body is the temple of the Holy Spirit who is in you, whom you have from God, and you are not your own? For you were bought at a price; therefore glorify God in your body and in your Spirit, which are God's.

- **UNDERSTAND.**

The Holy Spirit is often understood. People don't understand the Holy Spirit unless they are spiritual. How many times do we neglect the Holy Spirit and believe that he is going to cause us problems and most times he is always treated as something that we don't need. But still is not a thing but a person. Many people reject him because they don't understand him and they don't even want to know about him. But if you want to surrender or be a friend to the Holy Spirit, you have to understand his nature. If we want to walk with the Holy Spirit, we must understand him. Make him feel that he is at home and don't get ashamed of him.

- **TRUST HIM.**

Trust the Holy Spirit the way Jesus trusted him. Jesus trusted the Holy Spirit to raise him from the dead. In other words, he is the Holy Spirit who raised the son of God from the dead. **Roman 8:11** says, but if the spirit of him who raised Jesus from the dead dwells in you, he who raised Christ from the dead will also give life to your mortal bodies through his spirit who dwells in you.

- **COMMUNICATION.**

The Holy Spirit is always present. Since the Holy Spirit is always present, that means we can communicate with him from time to time, moment to moment and day by day. Communication is being aware of him. Be aware of him therefore think about him as often as possible in every circumstance. Let him help you, when you are tempted. He will deliver you from the power sin.

PRAYING IN THE SPIRIT.

Praying in the Spirit is praying secure between you and your heavenly father. **Matthew 6:5-8**. And when you pray, you shall not be like hypocrites. For they love to pray standing in the synagogues and on the corners of the streets, that they may be seen by men. Assuredly, I say to you, they have their reward. But you, when you pray, go into your room, and when you pray, go into your room and when you have shut your door, pray to your father who is in the secret place; and your father who is in the secret place will reward you openly. And when you pray, do not use vain repetitions as the heathen do. For they think that they will be heard for their many words. Therefore do not be like them. For your father knows the things you have need of before you ask him.

It is a gift to pray in the spirit that is received through faith in Christ Jesus. Praying in the spirit is praying with divine help. When you ask the Holy Spirit to guide you, you can pray in the spirit. When you have faith in God, trust in God and relay on God, you can pray in spirit. Still if you understand and act in the way God wants us to act, you can pray in the spirit and fellowship with the Holy Spirit

CHAPTER 2

GOD THE HOLY SPIRIT IN THE BIBLE.

We see the holy spirit in the book of **Number 27:18.** And the Lord said to Moses: "Take Joshua the son of Nun with you, a man in who are the spirit, and lay your hand on him.

Jesus promised a helper which is the Holy spirit to guide us always. And I will pray the Father, and he will give you another helper, that he may abide with you forever the spirit of truth, whom the world cannot receive, because it neither sees him nor knows him; but you know him, for he dwells with you and will be in you. I will not leave you orphans, I will come to you**. [John 14:16-18]**

The Holy Spirit who raised Jesus from the dead dwells in us, therefore we stay with the Holy Spirit. But if the spirit of him who raised Jesus from the dead dwells in you, he who raised Christ from the dead will also give life to your mortal bodies through his spirit who dwells in you**.[Romans 8:11]**

The Holy Spirit is the helper but doesn't want people who rebel against him. In their entire affliction he was afflicted, and the Angel of his presence saved them; in his love and in his pity he redeemed them; And he bore them and carried them All the days of old. But they rebelled and grieved his holy spirit; so he turned himself against them as an enemy, and he fought against them. Then he remembered the days of old, Moses and his people, saying:" where is he who brought them up out of the sea with the shepherd of his flock? Where is he who put his holy spirit within them**? [Isaiah 63:9-11]**

The Holy Spirit is into our hearts which means we were no longer a slaves but a son. **[Galatians 4:6-7]**; and because you are sons, God has sent forth the spirit of his son into your hearts, crying out, Abba, Father!"Therefore you are no longer a slave but a son, and if a son, then an heir of God through Christ.

According to **Genesis 1:2**, we see the spirit of God hovering over the face of the waters.

TRINITY IN THE BIBLE

Isaiah 48: 16-17." Come near to me, hear this: I have not spoken in secret from the beginning; from the time that it was there. And now the Lord God and his spirit have sent me." Thus says the Lord, your Redeemer, The holy one of Israel: " I am the LORD your God, who teaches you to profit, who leads you by the way you should go.

Revelation 1:7-8, presents the father and the son. Behold, He is coming with clouds, and every eye will see him, even they who pierced him. And all the tribes of the earth will mourn because of him. Even so, Amen. "I am the Alpha and the Omega, the beginning and the End,'' Says the Lord, who is and who was and who is to come, the Almighty."

In the book of John, we see the word being God and still the word becoming flesh. Jesus was the word that became flesh. In the beginning was the word, and the word was with God, and the word was God. **[John 1:1].** In **John 1:14**, the word became flesh and dwelt among us, and we beheld his glory as of the only begotten of the Father, full of grace and truth.

CHAPTER 3

GOD'S NAMES

God was a name from the German. The earliest written form of the Germanic word "God" comes from the 6th Century. The word God was used to represent Greek Theo's and Latin Deus in Bible translations, first in the Gothic translation of the New Testament by Ulfias. Christians believe God is a being that possesses the three necessary properties: Omniscience; which means he is all-knowing, He is Omnipotence; which means he is all powerful, and Omni benevolence; which means he is supremely good. Therefore God has power to do anything, knows everything and is perfectly good.

1] YAHWEH

Yahweh, the Israelites, whose name was revealed to Moses as four Hebrew consonants. Then Moses said to God, " indeed, when I come to the children of Israel and say to them, "The God of your fathers has sent me to you; and they say to me; what is him? What shall I say to them?" And God said to Moses, **"I AM WHO I AM"**. And he said, Thus you shall say to the children of Israel, ' I AM has sent me to you." Moreover God said to Moses, "Thus you shall say to the children of Israel : " The LORD God of your father, the God of Abraham, the God of Isaac, and the God of Jacob, has sent me to you. This is my name forever, and this is my memorial to all generations;

Exodus 3:13-15

2] ELOHIM

Elohim in scriptures is only found in the Hebrew translation. Elohim is the most frequently used name for God in scriptures. He is our creator." In the beginning God created the heavens and the earth.**" Genesis 1:1**. Have you ever thought of the power God used to create the universe? God's insanely creative imagination as he designed planet earth? Always in life don't forget to worship him always. **Genesis 1:27** "So God created man in his own image; in the image of God he created him; male and female he created them".

3] ELOHIM CHAYIM

He is the living God. "And Joshua said, by this you shall know that the living God is among you, and that he will without fail drive out from before you the Canaanites and Hittites and the Hivites and the Perizzites and the Girgashites and the Amorites and the Jebusites: " **[Joshua 3:10].**

1 Corinthians 15:3-7

Matthew 28:5-6

4] ABBA FATHER

He is our father **Romans 8:15.** For you did not receive the spirit of bondage again to fear, but you received the spirit of adoption by whom we cry out, "Abba, Father."

5] JEHOVAH JIREH

This is one of the most popular names of God. It means, "the Lord will provide". Genesis 22:9-14. Then they came to the place of which God had told him. And Abraham built an altar there and placed the wood in order; and he bound Isaac his son and laid him on the altar, upon the wood. And Abraham stretched out his hand and took the knife to slay his son. But the Angel of the LORD called to him from heaven and said, "Abraham, Abraham!"

So he said, "Here I am." And He said, "Do not lay your hand on the lad, or do anything to him; for now I know that you fear God, Since you have not withheld your son, your only son, from me." Then Abraham lifted his eyes and looked, and there behind him was a ram caught in a thicket by its horns. So Abraham went and took the ram, and offered it up for a burnt offering instead of his son. And Abraham called the name of the place, The LORD will provide; as it is said to this day, " In the mount of the LORD it shall be provided."

6] JEHOVAH SHALOM

"The LORD our peace". **JUDES 6:22-24**. Now Gideon perceived that he was the Angle of the LORD. So Gideon said. "Alas, O Lord God! For I have seen the Angel of the LORD face to face. Then the LORD said to him, peace be with you; do not fear, you shall not die. So Gideon built an altar there to the LORD, and called it The LORD- IS-PEACE. To this day it is still in Ophrah of the Abiezrites.

John 16:33. These things I have spoken to you, that in me you may have peace. In the world you will have tribulation; but be of good cheer, I have overcome the world."

7] EL ELYON

He is your Sovereign. He's in control of our lives and he has the right as God Almighty to do with our lives as he pleases. He is also referred to as God most high. **Genesis14:20**

8] EL KANNA

The jealous God. " You must worship no other gods, for the Lord, whose name is Jealous, is a God who is Jealous about his relationship with you"**. Exodus 34:14**. He wants nothing to take his place in our lives or in our hearts. You shall not bow down to them nor serve them. For I, the

LORD your God, am a jealous God, visiting the iniquity of the fathers upon the children to the third and fourth generations of those who hate me, but showing mercy to those who love me and keep my commandments. **Exodus 20:5-6**. Idolatry is on a high rate in today's world, so be aware of what you spend your time on , how you spend your time, what you think about also matters and what your hobbies and habits are. For where your treasure is, there your heart will be also. **Matthew 6:21**

9] El ROI

EL Roi is one of the names of God in the Hebrew Bible. It means, "the God who sees me". El ROI sees you and he cares. **Genesis 16:13** " Then she called the name of the LORD who spoke to her, you-are-the- God –who-sees; for she said, "Have I also here seen him who sees me?"

10] JEHOVAH RO'I

God is Jehovah RO'I. It means, " the Lord in my shepherd" and still known as Yahweh-Rohi. He is your shepherd. "The Lord is my shepherd, I shall not want". **Psalms 23:1**

11] JEHOVAH NISSI

God is Jehovah Nissi. He is my banner. " Moses built an altar there and named it Yahweh Nissi, which means the Lord is my banner" to celebrate the defeat of Amalekites at Rephidim. Banner meant deliverance and Salvation. The Lord will fight for us, the battle is his and he is a God of deliverances.

12] ALPHA AND OMEGA

" I am the Alpha and the Omega, the beginning and the End," says the Lord, who is and who was and who is to come, the Almighty**." Revelation 1:8**

13] ADONAI

This is the same as Lord in the Bible. "Master" or " Lord". **Judges 6: 15.**So he said to him, "O my Lord, how can I save Israel? Indeed my clan is the weakest in Manasseh, and I am the least in my father's house.". For I know that the LORD is great, and our Lord is above all gods. **Psalm 135:5**

Exodus 4:16

Psalm 114:7,

2 Samuel 7:18-20

1 Timothy 6:15

14] JEHOVAH ELOHIM

"Lord God"

This is the history of the heavens and earth when they were created, in the day that the LORD God made the earth and the heavens, before any plant of the field was in the earth and before any herb of the field had grown. For the LORD God had not caused it to rain on the earth, and there was no man to till the ground, but a mist went up from the earth and watered the whole face of the ground. **Genesis 2:4-6. Judges 5:3**

15] JEHOVAH ROPHE

He is our healer. He is always ready to you when you go to him. He is the perfect healer. Exodus 15:25-26.So he cried out to the LORD and the LORD showed him a tree. When he cast it into the waters, the waters were made sweet. There he made a statute and an ordinance for them, and there he tested them, and said, "if you diligently heed the voice of the LORD your God and do what is right in his sight, give ear to his commandments and keep all his statutes, I will put none of the diseases on you which I have brought on the Egyptians. For I am the LORD who heals you."

16] LORD OF HOSTS

Thus says the LORD of hosts: 'behold, I will save my people from the land of the east and from the land of the west; I will bring them back, and they shall dwell in the midst of Jerusalem. They shall be my people and I will be their God, in truth and righteousness.' **(Zechariah 8:7-8)**

And one cried to another and said: "Holy, holy, holy is the LORD of hosts; the whole earth is full of his glory!"**(Isaiah 6:3)**

For thus says the LORD of hosts" He sent me after glory, to the nations which plunder you; for he who touches you touches the apple of his eye. For surely I will shake my hand against them, and they shall become spoil for their servants. Then you will know that the LORD of hosts has sent me. **(Zechariah 2:8-9)**

CHAPTER 4

16 WAYS GOD SPEAKS TO US

- **THE BIBLE**

The Bible is a main way God speaks to us. God speaks to us when we read the bible on nearly every issue that applies to our way of living. Jesus taught us how to pray in **Matthew 6:11** and still Jesus tells us that whoever calls on his name, and asks in his name shall receive, seek and you shall find and also those that knock shall be opened. In **John 14:6,** Jesus said to him, " I am the way, the truth, and the life. No one comes to the father except through me." **Revelation 1:3**. Blessed is he who reads and those who hear the words of this prophecy, and keep those things which are written in it; for the time is near.

John 6:63. It is the spirit who gives life; the flesh profits nothing. The words that I speak to you are spirit, and they are life. **John 6:68.** But Simon Peter answered him," Lord, to whom shall we go? You have the words of eternal life.

- **AUDIBLE VOICE**

Through seemingly rare, God has and still can speak audibly. Adam and Eve heard God's voice in the Garden of Eden. And they heard the sound of the LORD God walking in the garden in the cool of the day, and Adam and his wife hid themselves from the presence of LORD God among the trees of the garden. Then the LORD God called to Adam and said to him, "where are you?" So he said, "I heard your voice in the garden, and I was afraid because I was naked; and I hid myself."**(Genesis 3:8-10).** God spoke audibly to Moses from the burning bush. So when the LORD saw that he turned aside to look, God called to him from the midst of the bush and said," Moses, Moses!" And he said, "Here I am." Then he said, "Do not draw near this place. Take your sandals off your feet, for the place where you stand is holy ground." Moreover he said, "I am the God of your father-the God of Abraham, the God of Isaac, and the God of Jacob." And Moses hid his face, for he was afraid to look upon God. (Exodus 3:4-6). And to all Israel from Mount Sinai. Then the LORD said to Moses, "thus you shall say to the children of Israel: 'You have seen that I have talked with you from heaven. **(Exodus 20:1-22).** And the LORD called Samuel again the third time. So he arose and went to Eli, and said, "here I am, for you did call me." Then Eli perceived that the LORD had called the boy. Therefore Eli said to Samuel, "Go, lie down; and it shall be, if he calls you, that you must say, speak, LORD, for your servant hears." So Samuel went and lady down in his place. Now the LORD came and stood and called as at other times, "Samuel! Samuel! "And Samuel answered," Speak, for your servant hears." Then the LORD said to Samuel: "Behold, I will do something in Israel at which both ears of everyone who hears it will tingle. **(Samuel 3:8-11)**

In the New Testament, the father endorsed Jesus at his baptism and his transfiguration with a literal Voice. And suddenly a voice came from heaven, saying, " this is my beloved son, in whom I am well pleased." **Matthew 3:17**

- **VISITATION OF ANGELS:**

God speaks to us through angels. Marry was visited by an angle before the birth of Jesus and even after the birth of Jesus. Joseph was also visited by an angle before marrying Marry. But while he thought about these things, behold, an angel of the Lord appeared to him in a dream, saying, "Joseph, son of David, do not be afraid to take to you Mary your wife, for that which is conceived in her is of the Holy Spirit. And she will bring forth a son, and you shall call his name JESUS, for he will save his people from their sins," **(Matthew 1:20-21)**. Angles are messengers on assignment sent to minister to heirs of salvation. There are numerous times in scripture where angles inform, warn or convey divine messages to individuals. In **Matthew 2:13** we see an angle appeared to Joseph in a dream saying, "Arise, take the young child and his mother, flee to Egypt, and stay there until I bring you word; for Herod will seek the young child to destroy him."

- **VISIONS**

A vision is an inspired appearance. Something you see literally with your eyes or in your mind or spirit. In the first year of Belshazzar king of Babylon, Daniel had a dream and a vision of his head while on his bed. Then he wrote down the dream, telling the main facts. Daniel spoke, saying, "I saw in my vision by night, and behold; the four winds of heaven were stirring up the Great sea. And four great beasts came up from the sea, each different from the other. The first was like a lion, and had eagle's wings. I watched till its wings were plucked off; and it was lifted up from the earth and made to stand on two feet like a man, and a man's heart was given to it.

"And suddenly another beast, a second, like a bear. It was raised up on one side, and had three ribs in its mouth between its teeth. And they said thus to it: Arise, devour much flesh!' "After this I looked, and there was another, like a leopard, which had on its back four wings of a bird. The beast also had four heads, and dominion was given to it.

"After this I saw in the night visions, and behold, a fourth beast, dreadful, a fourth beast, dreadful and terrible, exceedingly strong. It had huge iron teeth; it was devouring breaking in pieces, and trampling the residue with its feet. It was different from all the beasts that were before it, and it had ten horns. I was considering the horns, and there was another horn, a little one, coming up among them, before whom three of the first horns were plucked out by the roots. And there, in this horn, were eyes like the eyes of a man, and a mouth speaking pompous words. "I watched till thrones were put in place, And the ancient of days was seated; his garment was white as snow, and the hair of his head was like pure wool. **(Daniel 7:1-9).** And it shall come to pass in the last days, says God, That I will pour out of my spirit on all flesh; your sons and your daughters shall prophesy, your young men shall see visions, your old men shall dream dreams.

- **DREAMS**

A dream is something seen in your sleep in your sleep or something you imagine doing and ideals into our minds whether we are conscious or not. **Genesis 40:5-13**. Then the butler and the baker of the king of Egypt, who were confined in the prison, had a dream, both of them, each man's dream with its own interpretation. And Joseph came in to them in the morning and looked at them, and saw that they were sad. So he asked Pharaoh's officers who were with him the Custody of his Lord's house, saying, "why do you look so sad today?" And they said to him, we each have had a dream, and there is no interpreter of it."

So Joseph said to them, Do not interpretations belong to God? Tell them to me, please." Then the chief butler told his dream to Joseph, and said to him, "Behold, in my dream a vine was before me, and in the vine were three branches; it was as though it budded, its blossoms shot forth ripe grapes. Then Pharaoh's cup was in my hands; and I took the grapes and pressed them into Pharaoh's cup, and placed the cup in Pharaoh's hand." And Joseph said to him, "this is the interpretation of it: The three branches are three days. Now within three days Pharaoh will lift up your head and restore you to your place, and you will put Pharaoh's cup in his hand according to the former manner, when you were his butler. **Matthew 1:20, Matthew 2:13, Matthew 2:19.**

- **SIGNS**

God also provides signs to people. People also ask signs from God which is okay but still it depends on your motive. Luke 23:8- Some people who asked Jesus for a miracle just for him to prove his divinity were denied, but those who asked for a sign to confirm his will were often rewarded.

Luke 23:8-11. Now when Herod saw Jesus, he was exceedingly glad; for he had desired for a long time to see him, because he had heard many things about him, and he hoped to see some miracle done by him. Then he questioned him with many words, but he answered him nothing. And the chief priests and scribes stood and vehemently accused him. Then Herod, with his men of war, treated him with contempt and mocked him, arrayed him in a gorgeous robe, and sent him back to Pilate.

Gideon put a fleece out sincerely seeking confirmation of God's will and was answered. **(Judges 6:36-40).**

- **HOLY SPIRIT**

God often speaks to us though the inner witness which is the Holy Spirit to our Spirit. For as many as are led by the spirit of God, these are sons of God. For you did not receive the spirit of bondage again to fear, but you received the spirit of adoption by whom we cry, "Abba, Father." The Spirit himself bears witness with our spirit that we are children of God, and if children, then heirs-heirs of God and joint heirs with Christ, if indeed we suffer with him, that we may also be glorified together. **Romans 8:14-17**

- **THROUGH PRAYER**

Prayer is the way to the supernatural and spiritual realm. Once you start to pray and focus on God to lead you, then God will lead you in whatever you do and you can feel his presence. It hard to understand it because it may not make sense to you but the Holy spirit guides us and teaches us how to pray. Likewise the spirit also helps in our weaknesses. For we do not know what we should pray for as we ought, but the spirit himself makes intercession for us with groaning which cannot be uttered. Now he who searches the hearts knows what the mind of the spirit is, because he makes intercession for the saints according to the will of God. **Romans 8:26-27**

- **COINCIDENCES**

Sometimes God speaks to us through coincidences. For example when we look at what happened to Job. In **Job 1-2,** Job the man who was blameless and upright, and the one who feared God and shunned evil, was attacked by Satan and lost everything that he had but still Job remained faithful to God.

- **THROUGH PEOPLE**

God speak through preachers and teachers but he can also speak through spouse, friends, kids and even enemies. **1 Corinthians 12: 7-10.** But the manifestation of the spirit is given to each one for the profit of all: for to one is given the word of wisdom through the spirit, to another the word of knowledge through the same spirit, to another faith by the same spirit, to another gifts of healings by the same spirit, to another prophecy, to another discerning of spirits, to another different kinds of tongues, to another the interpretation of tongues. If anyone speaks, let him speak as oracles of God. If anyone ministers, let him do it as with the ability which God supplies, that in all things God may be glorified through Jesus Christ, to whom belong the glory and the dominion forever and ever. Amen. **1 Peter 4:11**

- **THROUGH CREATION AND NATURE**

The heavens declare the glory of God; and the firmament shows his handwork. Day unto day utters speech and night unto night reveals knowledge. There is no speech nor language where their voice is not heard. Their line has gone out through all the earth and their words to the end of the world. In them he set a tabernacle for the sun, which is like a bridge groom coming out his Chamber, and rejoices like a strong man to run its race. Its rising is from one end of heaven, and its circuit to the other end; and there is nothing hidden from its heat. The law of the LORD is perfect, converting the soul; The testimony of the LORD is sure, making wise the simple; The statutes of the LORD are right ,rejoicing the heart; The commandment of the LORD is pure, enlightening the eyes; The fear of the LORD is clean, enduring forever; The judgments of the LORD are true and righteous altogether. **Psalms 19:1-9**

- **GOD'S STILL SMALL VOICE**

God also speaks to us using his still small voice as he did to Elijah. **1 kings 19:9-16**. And there he went into a cave, and spent the night in that place; and behold, the word of the LORD came to him, and he said to him, " what are you doing here, Elijah?" So he said, "I have been very zealous for the LORD God of hosts; for the children of Israel have forsaken your Covenant, torn down your altars, and killed your prophets with the sword. I alone am left; and they seek to take my life."

Then he said, " Go out, and stand on the mountain before the LORD." And behold, the LORD passed by, and a great and strong wind tore into the mountains and broke the rocks in pieces before the LORD, but the LORD was not in the wind; and after the wind an earthquake, but the LORD was not in the earthquake; and after the earthquake a fire, but the LORD was not in the fire; and after the fire a still small voice. So it was, when Elijah heard it, that he wrapped his face in his mantle and went out and stood in the entrance of the cave. Suddenly a voice came to him, and said," What are you doing here**,** Elijah?" And he said, "I have been very zealous for the LORD God of hosts; because the children of Israel have forsaken your covenant, torn down your altars, and killed your prophets with the sword. I alone am left; and they seek to take my life." Then the LORD said to him; "Go, return on your way to the wilderness of Damascus; and when you arrive, anoint Hazael as king over Syria. Also you shall anoint Jehu the son of Nimshi as king over Israel. And Elisha the son of Shaphat of Abel Meholah you shall anoint as prophet in your place.

- **THROUGHOURCONSCIENCE.**

God gave us the inner awareness of what is right and wrong with an inclination to do right. Even if you have never read the Ten Commandments, you may have that in your minds that stealing is wrong, murder is bad, committing adultery is wrong and bearing false witness against your neighbor is bad. But still also you grow up knowing that it's good to love and to be loved. No one teaches a baby to love the parents but because it's a gift from God, we all have to love and we all know how it feels like to be loved. But still we know its right to love. And still it's a free will.

- **THROUGH MUSIC**

God communicates through the gospel songs. This is one of the most common in most people's relationship with God. God will do anything to catch your attention. A random song will drop in your spirit and it will be exactly the word you need in that time. A song may come as a confirmation, a prophecy and a warning.

- **THROUGH REPEATED INSTANCES**

Sometimes when similar things repeatedly occur over a space of time, it might be a call from God for your attention. It may be a warning from God, so always does not take that for granted.

- **THROUGH MIRACLES**

This can also be called Supernatural manifesting .God sometime speaks through miracles. He always use the miracles mainly to increase our faith, to give hope to us and for his glory. Jesus walks on the water. **John 6:15-21**. Jesus feeds the five thousand people. **John 6:1-14.**

- **HOLY SPIRIT VOICE**

This is in God's word and God's nature. But God has revealed to them to us through his spirit. For the spirit it searches all things, yes, and the deep things of God. **1 Corinthians 2:10.** My sheep hear my voice, and I know them, and they follow me. And I give them eternal life, and they shall never perish; neither shall anyone snatch them out of my father's hand. **John 10:27-29.** Still the Holy Spirit is a teacher. These things that we also speak, not words which man's wisdom teaches but which the holy spirit teaches, comparing spiritual things with spiritual. **1 Corinthians 2:13.**

e?" And he said, "who are you, Lord?" Then the Lord said, "I am Jesus, whom you are persecuting. It is hard for you to kick against the goads." So he, trembling and astonished, said, "Lord, what do you want me to do? Then the Lord said to him, "Arise and go into the city, and you will be told what you must do." God chose Saul to be his vessel to bear his name before Gentile, kings, and the children of Israel. And he was to be shown many things to suffer for God's sake**. Acts 9.**

Stop leaving out for someone's purpose for Peter and Apostle Paul were all evangelism but everyone had to do it in their only way. So stop comparing yourself to others. Stop finding your purpose based on what you see other people doing. Listen to the voice of the Holy Spirit, not what other people are saying.

If you look at someone's calling and you wonder why it is so beautiful and you compare to your own, then the problem is that you haven't considered the creator who is the painter. God has painted the picture of your life and he has said that it good and he has said that its good and he loves it. Instead of telling him that he messed up on the painting, wake up and ask him to tell you more about the painting.

GOD'S GIFTS

Every person who was created in this world has a gift that God gave him. Since everyone has a call in this world, also God gave us gifts to fulfill our calls. Serve God with spiritual gifts.

- **LEADERSHIP**

Some people have that gift of leadership in that they can be followed by so many people. Such people who have that gift of leadership can use it to lead the people the people to God.

- **CONTRIBUTING TO THE NEEDS OF OTHERS WITH CHEERFULNESS AND GENEROSITY**

For as we have many members in one body, but all the members do not have the same function, so we, being many, are one body in Christ, and individually members of one another. Having then gifts differing according to the grace that is given to us, let us use them: if prophecy, let us prophesy in proportion to our faith; or ministering; he who teaches, in teaching; he who exhorts, in exhortation; he who leads, with diligence; he who shows mercy, with cheerfulness. **Roman 12:4-8.**

- **ENCOURAGEMENT**

There are people who are gifted with the gift of encouragement. Such people are good at encouraging others. **Romans 12:4-8**

- **EVANGELISM**

He who descended far above all the heavens, that he might fill all things.) And he himself gave some to be apostles, some prophets, some evangelists, and some pastors and teachers, for the equipping of the saints for the work of ministry, for the edifying of the body of Christ, till we all come to the unity of the faith and of the knowledge of the son of God, to a perfect man, to the measure of the stature of the fullness of Christ; that we should no longer be children, tossed to and fro and carried about with every wind of doctrine, by the trickery of men, in the cunning craftiness of deceitful plotting, but, speaking the truth in love, may grow up in all things into him who is the head-Christ-from whom the body, joined and knit together by what every joint supplies, according to the effective working by which every part does its share, causes growth of the body for the edifying of itself in love. **Ephesians 4:10-16**

- **FAITH**

There people who have the gift of faith. According to 1 Corinthians 12:9, the manifestation of the spirit of God it is given to each one for the profit of all: people are given the gift of faith.

- **WISDOM**

There are diversities of gift, but the same spirit, there are differences of ministries, but the same Lord. And there are diversities of activities, but it is the same God who works all in all: But the manifestation of the spirit it is given to each one for the profit of all: for to one is given the word of wisdom through the spirit. **1 Corinthians 12:4-8.**

- **KNOWLEDGE**

Other people are given the gift of knowledge. Such people can also use the knowledge which God gave them to help the others to glorify God. The spirit of God gives the gift of knowledge. **1 Corinthians 12:8**

- HEALINGS

There are some people who are given the gift of healing. Such people pray for theirs and they get healed. **1 Corinthians 12:9**

- **WORKING MIRACLES**

The spirit of God gives the gift of working miracles. 1 Corinthians 12:10

- **PROPHECY**

Not everyone can prophecy. It is a gift given to the people by the spirit of God. So such people are called to be prophets and prophecy in the name of God. 1 Corinthians 12:10

- **DIFFERENT KINDS OF TONGUES**

People are given different gifts. There are people who are gifted with different kinds of tongues. They can talk in languages and this can help in preaching the gospel in different parts of the world. 1Corinthians12:10

- **INTERPRETATION OF TONGUES**

The spirit of God gives the gift of interpreting tongues. This gift helps in letting people from different parts of the world to know more about God. 1 Corinthians 12:10

- **DISCERNING OF SPIRITS**

There are other people who are God gives them the spirit of discerning of spirit. **1Cornithian12:10**

- **HELPING OTHERS**

Now you are the body of Christ, and members individually. And God has appointed these in the church: fist apostles, second prophets, third teachers, after that miracle, then gifts of healings, helps, administrations, and varieties of tongues. **1 Corinthians13:27-28**

- **LOVE**

This is given to everyone. Every person has this gift of love. If you love then it's easy to fulfill God's law. Love suffers long and is kind; love does not envy; love does not parade itself, is not puffed up; does not behave rudely, does not seek its own, is not provoked, thinks no evil; does not rejoice in iniquity, but rejoices in the truth, bears all things, believes all things, hopes all things, endures all things. Love never fails. But whether there are prophecies, they will fail;

whether there are tongues, they will cease; whether there is knowledge, it will vanish away. **1 Corinthians 13:4-8.**

- **PEACE**

Peace is one of the gifts that the Holy Spirit gives to the people.

CHAPTER 6

HOW TO GET TO KNOW YOUR PURPOSE

The purpose is always connected to your calling. Before we understand our purposes, we are called to live a Christian life. God reveals our calling through the following.

- **THROUGH SCRPITURE (READING THE BIBLE)**

The primary way God speaks to us is through the Bible. This means that one of the first things you should do in your life is to read the scriptures.

Jesus said it in **Mark 16:15-16**. And he said to them, ''go into the entire world and preach the gospel to every creature. He who believes and is baptized will be saved; but he who does not believe will be condemned.

We always think it is connected to the talents, gifts, intelligence but the truth is God can use those things, he doesn't discount them but he is not limited by them.

I always hear people who hear a prophetic word about their purpose but then after sometime they ran from that word, but the problem is, when we ran from his word whether its written word or the leading of the Holy Spirit, we ran from his presence. **Psalms 119:105.** Your word is a lamp to my feet and a light to my path.

- **THROUGH GOD'S VOICE**

- Paul the apostle hatred Christians and killed them. He went to their houses drag them from their house and take them to jail but Jesus called him and changed him with his voice. His name was Saul but later changed to Paul. Then Saul, still breathing threats and murder against the disciples of the Lord, went to the high priest and asked letters from him to the synagogues of Damascus, so that if he found any who were of the way, whether men or women, he might bring them bound to Jerusalem. As he journey he came near Damascus, and suddenly a light shone around him from heaven. Then he fell to the ground, and heard a voice saying to him, "Saul, Saul, why are persecuting m

Trust in the LORD with all your heart, and lean not on your own understanding; in all your ways acknowledge him, and he shall direct your paths. **Proverbs 3:5-6**. When you are trying to get to know your life purpose, you can be stressful. It looks to be confusing and frustrating. You want to steep in your calling but you're not sure how to do it. You want to find your purpose but you feel you're messing up. But then you have to trust God to show you the reason why he created you. Do not be wise in your own eyes; fear the LORD and depart from evil. **Proverbs 3:7.**

- **GOD CAN USE PEOPLE TO TELL YOU HIS PURPOSE**

God can reveal to you the purpose to you through different people but the difficult thing to notice from them is the message of the gospel. A wise man will hear and increase learning, and a man of understanding will attain wise counsel. **Proverbs 1:5**

- **ALLOW GODTO EMPOWER YOUIN YOUR PURPOSE.**

You have to be ready to stand in God's presence. Many people are missing their purpose not because they are running from their calling but because they are actually running from the presence of God. We see Jonah running away from God just because he never wanted to be a messenger. **Jonah 1:3**

The problem we ran away from God and we decided to do what we want. **1 Corinthians 12:3-5.** Therefore I make known to you that no one speaking by the spirit of God calls Jesus is Lord expect by the Holy Spirit. There are diversities of gifts, but the same spirit. There are differences of ministries, but the same Lord. **1 Corinthians 12:7.** But the manifestation of the spirit is given to each one for the profit of all. The LORD is my shepherd; I shall not want. He makes me to lie down in green pastures; he leads me beside the still waters. He restores my soul; he leads me in the paths of righteousness for his name's sake. **Psalm 23:1-3**

- **TO KNOW GOD AND WALK WITH HIM.**

The great purpose is us to know God and walk with him. The truth is even though you get to enjoy your purpose through what you do, you can't find your purpose in what you do, you must find your purpose in who you know. Check yourself, are you focused on Jesus or not? So then, those who are in the flesh cannot please God. But you are not in flesh but in the spirit, if indeed the spirit of God dwells in you. Now if anyone does not have the spirit of Christ, he is not his. And if Christ is in you, the body is dead because of sin, but the spirit is life because of righteousness. But if the spirit of him who raised Jesus from the dead dwells in you, He who raised Christ from the dead will also give life to your mortal bodies through his spirit who dwells in you. **Romans 8:8-11**

- **KNOW YOUR GIFTS AND STRENGTH**

God has given you specific gifts and strength. Gifts like leadership, evangelism, help, hospitality, teaching, patience, knowledge, peace, wisdom and distinguishing spirits. Therefore you are supposed to use those gifts that God gave you so that you can do your purpose on earth. God's purpose for you probably involves the things you're already good at.

- **KNOW YOURPASSIONS.**

If you determine your passions often, this will help you know what God has called you to do. It is important for you to know your gifts and passions because you may find out that where your gifts meets your passions, that may be God's purpose for you. So you better know your passion.

- **ALLOW OTHER PEOPLE INTO YOUR LIFE.**

People who you trust can be your counselors. This may be your parent, friend or spouses. Really you need wise counselors to help you find God's purpose for you. These people should be the people who always have your back and want the best for you.

- **ALLOW THE HOLY SPIRIT TO LEAD YOU.**

If you want to know your purpose, allow the Holy Spirit to lead you**. Romans 8:14**. For as many are lead by the Spirit of God, these are sons of God. For you did not receive the spirit of bondage again to fear, but you received the spirit of adoption by whom we cry out, Abba, Father." **John 14:26.** But the helper, the holy spirit, whom the father will send in my name, He will teach you all things, and bring to your remembrance all things that I said to you. The Holy Spirit is not only a personal guide but also a teacher in this life so allow him to lead you.

- **DO NOT FOCUSS ON DISTRACTIONS.**

In this world, it's so easy to get distracted but if we want to fulfill God's calling for our lives, we must refuse to be distracted.1 Timothy 4:16. Take heed to yourself and to the doctrine. Continue in them, for in doing this you will save both yourself and those who hear you.

- **KNOW WHO YOU ARE INCHRIST.**

It's good to know who you are in Jesus Christ. Follow him and his examples. Your purpose as a believer is to build the kingdom of God. Your role in his kingdom will require your natural gifts and talents. **Ephesians 1:17-18.**That the God of our Lord Jesus Christ, the father of glory, may give to you the spirit of wisdom and revelation in the knowledge of him, the eyes of your understanding being enlightened; that you may know what is the hope of his calling, what are the riches of the glory of his inheritance in the saints. **1Timothy 6:12.** Fight the good fight of faith, lay hold on eternal life, to which you were also called and have confessed the good confession in the presence of many witnesses.

- **INCREASE YOUR FAITH IN GOD**

Faith is everything. Everything that God promised us, we get them just because we have faith. **Roman 12:3.** For I say, through the grace given to me, to everyone who is among you, not to think of himself more highly than he ought to think, but to think soberly, as God has dealt to each one a measure of faith. Without faith it is impossible to please God. Faith is the means by which we export heavenly goods and import them in our lives. Therefore if'

CHAPTER 7

BLASPHEMY

Blasphemy of the Holy Spirit is mentioned in three of our four gospels. It is found in Mathew 12:22-32; Mark 33:22-30 and again in Luke 12:10. The consequence of blaspheming the Holy Spirit is death.

Luke 12:10

And everyone who speaks a word against the son of man will be forgiven, but the one who blasphemes against the Holy Spirit will not be forgiven.

Mark 3:29

" Truly, i say to you, all sin will be forgiven the children of man, and whatever blasphemies they utter, But whoever blasphemes against the Holy Spirit never has forgiveness, but is guilty of an eternal sin".

Matthew 12:31-32

Therefore i tell you, every sin and blasphemy will be forgiven people, but the blasphemy against the Holy Spirit will not be forgiven. And whoever speaks against the Holy Spirit will not be forgiven, either in this age or in the age to come.

Exodus 20:7

"You shall not take the name of the Lord your God in vain, for the Lord will not hold him guiltless who takes his name in vain.

Leviticus 24:16

Whoever blasphemes the name of the LORD shall surely be put to death. All congregation shall stone him.

5 SIGNS YOU HAVE THE HOLY SPIRIT IN YOU.

1] MATURE AS BELIEVERS

Holy Spirit helps us mature as believers, and brings about transformation of our hearts and minds. Titus3:4-6 clearly shows this. "But when the kindness and the love of God our savior towards man appeared, not by works of righteousness when we have done ,but according to his mercy he saved us, through the washing of regeneration and renewing of the Holy Spirit, whom he poured out on us abundantly.

2] LEAD OF THE HOLY SPIRIT

When a believer is led by the Holy Spirit, they will obey God's word, and go in the direction that he wants them to go. "For as many are led by the Spirit of God, these are sons of God". [Romans 8:14.

3] SPEAKING IN TONGUES.

Acts 2:4 "And they were all filled with the Holy Spirit and began to speak with other tongues, as the spirit gave them utterance". Also in Mark 16: 17, it's also clear. 'In my name they will speak with new tongues".

4] TESTING THE SPIRITS

"Beloved, doesn't believe every Spirit, but test the spirits, whether they are of God; because many false prophets have gone out into the world." 1 John 4:1

5] HAVING FRUITS OF THE HOLY SPIRIT.

"But the fruit of the Spirit is love, joy, peace, long suffering, kindness, goodness, faithfulness, gentleness, self-control. Against such there is no law." Galatians 5:22-23.

CHAPTER 8

30 THINGS THE HOLY SPIRIT DOES

1] HELPS US [Romans 8:26]

2] He teaches us [john 14:26]

3] He guides us [john 16:13]

4] He calls us [Acts 13:2]

5] He bears witness to the truth [Roman [

6] He Reveals [1 corinthians2:10]

7] He comforts us [Acts 9:31]

8] He speaks [Revelation 2:7]

9] He fills us [Acts 4:31]

10] He testifies of Jesus Christ [John 15:26]

11] He strengthens us [Ephesians 3:16]

12] He instructs [Acts 8:29]

13] He prays for us [Romans 8:26]

14] He prophesies through us [Revelation 22:17]

15] He frees us [Romans 8:2]

16] He helps us to obey [1 peter 1:22]

17] He gives gifts [1 Corinthians 12:8-10]

18] He empowers us [Acts 1:8]

19] He unites us [Ephesians 4:3-4]

20] He transforms us [2 Corinthians3:18]

21] He lives in us [1 Corinthians 3:16]

22] He sanctifies us [2 Thessalonians 1:6]

23] He leads us [Romans 8:14]

24] He convicts of sin [John 16:8]

25] He brings freedom [2 Corinthians 3

26] He renews us [Titus 3:5]

27] He seals us [Ephesians 1:13]

28] He casts out Demons [Matthew 12:28]

29] He enables us to wait [Galatians5:5]

30] He gives us access to the father[Ephesians 2:18]

www.ingramcontent.com/pod-product-compliance
Lightning Source LLC
LaVergne TN
LVHW060508170826
845677LV00026B/1658
9798370509377